For Patty,
50 years my guiding star. —J. S.

For Jonathan Struan,
happy first birthday, love from Alison. —A. J.

G. P. PUTNAM'S SONS
A division of Penguin Young Readers Group
Published by The Penguin Group
Penguin Group (USA) Inc., 375 Hudson Street, New York, NY 10014, U.S.A.
Penguin Group (Canada), 10 Alcorn Avenue, Toronto, Ontario, Canada M4V 3B2
(a division of Pearson Penguin Canada Inc.).
Penguin Books Ltd, 80 Strand, London WC2R 0RL, England.
Penguin Ireland, 25 St. Stephen's Green, Dublin 2, Ireland (a division of Penguin Books Ltd.).
Penguin Group (Australia), 250 Camberwell Road, Camberwell, Victoria 3124, Australia (a division of Pearson Australia Group Pty Ltd).
Penguin Books India Pvt Ltd, 11 Community Centre, Panchsheel Park, New Delhi – 110 017, India.
Penguin Group (NZ), Cnr Airborne and Rosedale Roads, Albany, Auckland 1310, New Zealand
(a division of Pearson New Zealand Ltd).
Penguin Books (South Africa) (Pty) Ltd, 24 Sturdee Avenue, Rosebank, Johannesburg 2196, South Africa.
Penguin Books Ltd, Registered Offices: 80 Strand, London WC2R 0RL, England.

Text copyright © 2005 by Joseph Slate. Illustrations copyright © 2005 by Alison Jay.
All rights reserved. This book, or parts thereof, may not be reproduced in any form without permission in writing
from the publisher, G. P. Putnam's Sons, a division of Penguin Young Readers Group, 345 Hudson Street, New York, NY 10014.
G. P. Putnam's Sons, Reg. U.S. Pat. & Tm. Off. The scanning, uploading and distribution of this book via the Internet
or via any other means without the permission of the publisher is illegal and punishable by law.
Please purchase only authorized electronic editions, and do not participate in or encourage electronic piracy
of copyrighted materials. Your support of the author's rights is appreciated.
Published simultaneously in Canada. Manufactured in China by South China Printing Co. Ltd.
Designed by Marikka Tamura. Text set in Steam.
The art was done in Alkyd oil paint with crackling varnish.
Library of Congress Cataloging-in-Publication Data
Slate, Joseph. What star is this? / Joseph Slate ; illustrated by Alison Jay.
p. cm. Summary: A small comet heads for earth and arrives at the manger where Baby Jesus lies.
1. Jesus Christ—Nativity—Juvenile fiction. [1. Jesus Christ—Nativity—Fiction. 2. Comets—Fiction. 3. Stories in rhyme.]
I. Jay, Alison, ill. II. Title. PZ8.3.S629Wg 2005 [E]—dc22 2004004981 ISBN 0-399-24014-4
1 3 5 7 9 10 8 6 4 2
First Impression

What Star Is This?

JOSEPH SLATE · ILLUSTRATED BY ALISON JAY

G. P. PUTNAM'S SONS · NEW YORK

Far off in space where comets fly

in an icy ring through the deep dark sky,

a tiny comet with a budding tail

is born this night on that frosty trail.

What star is this?

It bounces off its icy berth

and sails away for the far~off earth.

Down, down—its beam is on the dancing Goat and the gliding Swan,

the dipping Bear, the leaping Lion, the flying Horse, and the hunter Orion.

What star is this?

Planets pull and meteors fly,

but the bold little comet ducks right by.

On and on its glowing sail

spreads out like a peacock's tail.

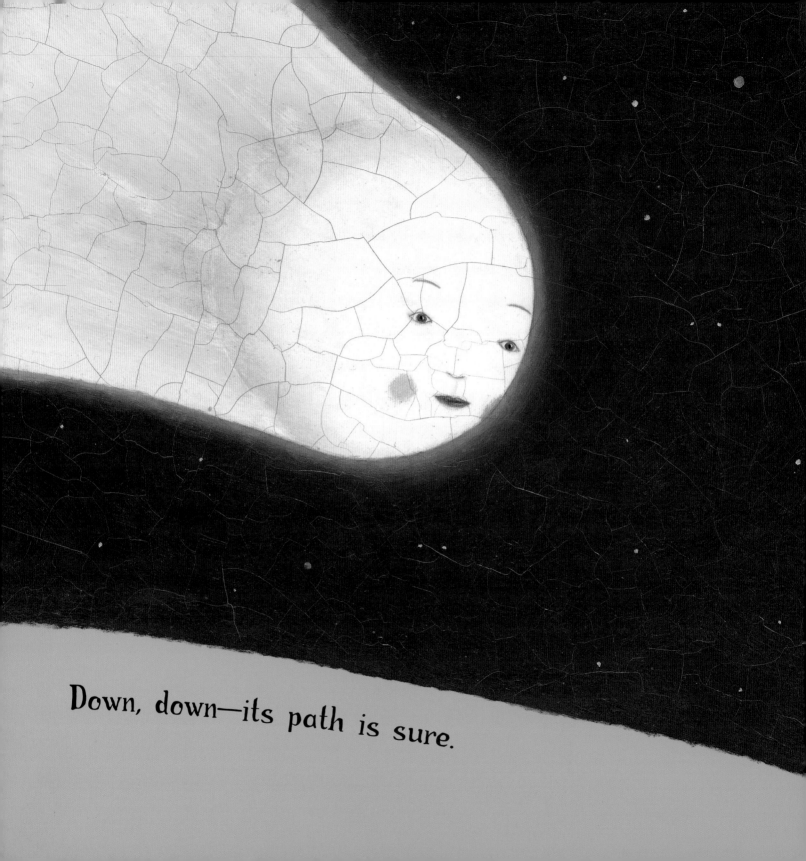

Down, down—its path is sure.

It knows the One it's headed for.

Then over the earth, asleep and still,

the comet blinks, "Good will! Good will!"

And far below, wise men cry,

"What star is this that lights the sky?"

Then suddenly at birth of day,
shepherds hear the angels say:

"Go to the manger! Have no care!
For see, the Star you want is there!"

And there He is,
in Mary's bed,
a glowing ring
around his head.

"What star is this?" They kneel to see.

The Baby Jesus—it is He!